What's it made from?

Clothes	2
Glass	4
Metal	6
Plastic	10
Mixing components	14
"Green" substances	16
Smart fabrics	20
Fabrics	22

Written by Isabel Thomas

Collins

Some clothes are special. They help people excel at difficult and dangerous jobs!

Each outfit is made with the best thing for the job.

Did you know that clothes can be made from glass, metal, plastic and ... nettles?

2

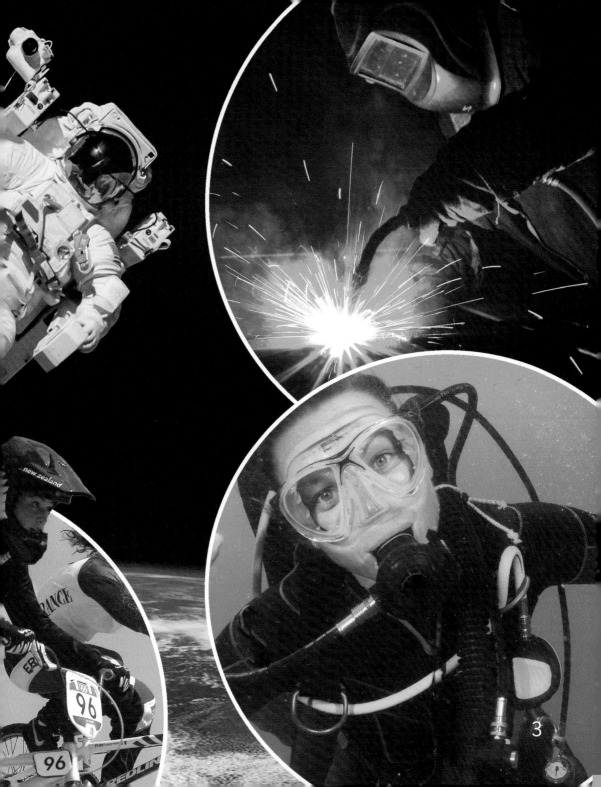

Glass

Welders join pieces of metal together using heat.
Welding helmets have a transparent glass visor.
It is heat resistant – it won't catch fire if a spark hits it.

Metal

Motorcycle racers whizz around corners at speed.

Sometimes their knees touch the ground!

Their clothes have metal plates hidden inside.

If the racer falls off, the strong metal will protect their skin.

steel knee protection

Volcanologists are scientists who study volcanoes.
Volcanoes are hot and release toxic gasses
into the atmosphere.

A proximity suit is essential for getting close to a volcano.

The shiny foil fabric reflects heat away from the volcanologists.

If there is an explosion of hot ash, the metal fabric will not catch fire.

Plastic

Cyclists wear helmets to protect their heads. Helmet designers use plastic to balance strength with lightness.

Plastic foam is full of air pockets. It crushes easily if it hits the ground, absorbing energy from a fall.

Spacesuits could get damaged by orbiting space junk. To protect themselves from danger, astronauts wear layers of plastic fabrics.

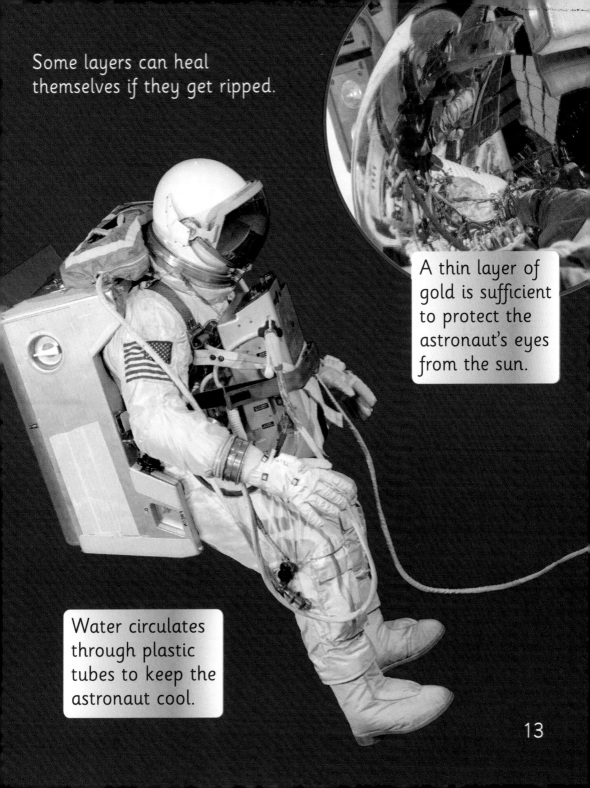

Some layers can heal themselves if they get ripped.

A thin layer of gold is sufficient to protect the astronaut's eyes from the sun.

Water circulates through plastic tubes to keep the astronaut cool.

Mixing components

Wetsuits help people to stay warm in the water, especially for sports like surfing.

Wetsuits use a mixture of plastic foam, water and metal.

The foam is stretchy, so the surfer can move their limbs, and stops heat from escaping.

There is shiny metal inside the wetsuit, which reflects heat back to the body.

"Green" substances

Scientists are on a mission to find new fabrics that are kinder to the planet. Would you wear clothes made from stinging nettles?

That sounds unusual, but it's not a trick question! Nettle plants grow quickly, require less water than cotton plants and the fabric is stronger.

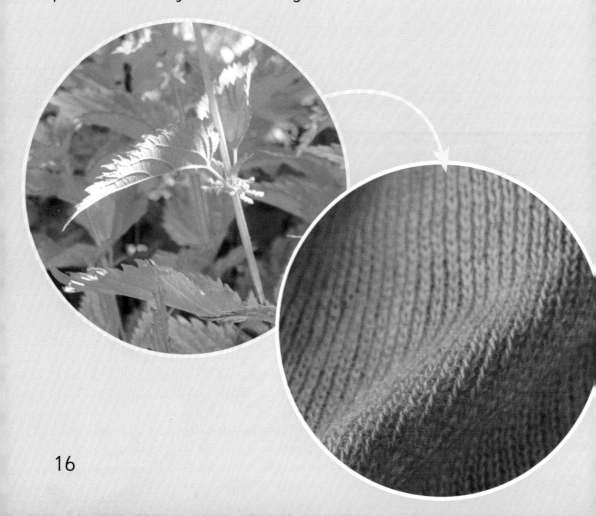

Bamboo fibres pull moisture away from the skin to keep the body dry.

Bamboo is one of the fastest growing plants in the world, and decomposes faster than plastic.

What about fabric made from slime?

Hagfish make stretchy slime to defend themselves.

Hagfish slime has special properties. It contains thousands of tiny, strong threads, which can be used to make unbreakable, stretchy fibres.

In the future, these could replace plastic fibres such as nylon.

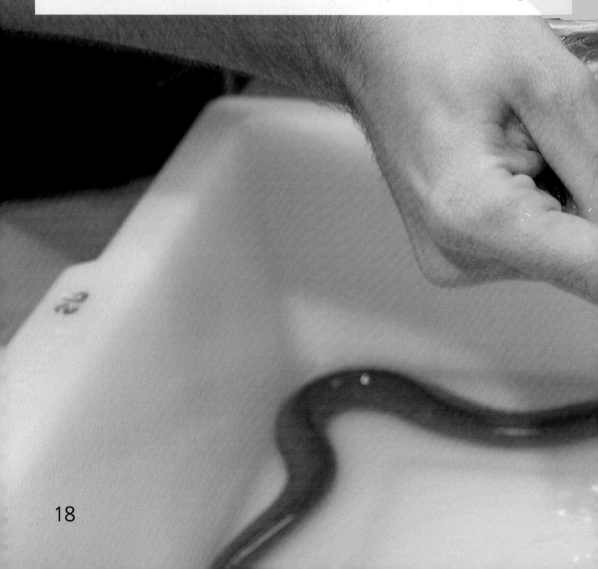

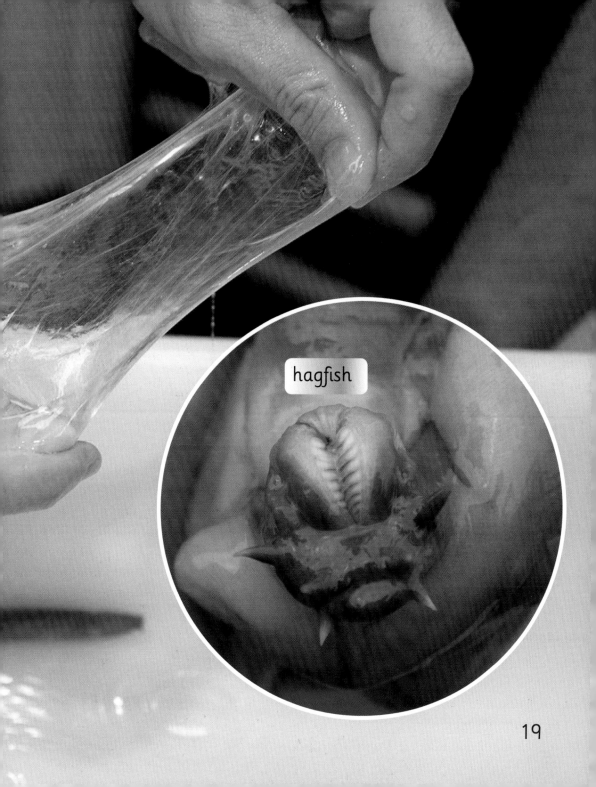

hagfish

19

Smart fabrics

In the future, clothes will be made from a mixture of things.

Scientists have invented fabrics with electronics woven in.

They could be used for communication, or to change our appearance.

Other smart fabrics can measure body heat and motion, collect information about how we're feeling and help to keep us healthy.

In the future, our clothes will be as unique as we are!

Fabrics

Glass	Metal	Plastic
	 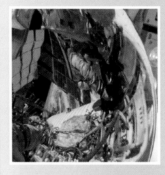 	 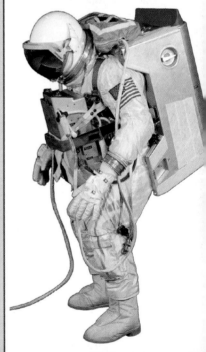

Mixture

Green

Smart

23

After reading

Letters and Sounds: Phases 5–6

Word count: 500

Focus phonemes: /n/ kn, gn /m/ mb /sh/ ci, ti, si, ssi /s/ c, ce, sc /c/ qu(e) /zh/ s

Common exception words: of, to, the, into, are, so, one, our, their, people, break (unbreakable), water, who, move, eyes

Curriculum links: Science: Everyday materials

National Curriculum learning objectives: Spoken language: articulate and justify answers, arguments and opinions; Reading/word reading: read common exception words, noting unusual correspondences between spelling and sound and where these occur in the word; read words containing taught GPCs and –s, –es, –ing, –ed, –er and –est endings; Reading/comprehension: understand both the books they can already read accurately and fluently and those they listen to by checking that the text makes sense to them as they read, and correcting inaccurate reading

Developing fluency
- Your child may enjoy hearing you read the book.
- You may wish to take turns to read a page. Alternatively, you could read out the main text and your child could read out the fact boxes.

Phonic practice
- Talk about how the same sound can be written in different ways. Focus on the /n/ sound in the following words:

  know   designers   nettles
- Ask your child to sound out and blend each word:

  kn/ow   d/e/s/i/gn/e/r/s   n/e/tt/le/s
- Talk about the different ways that the /n/ sound is spelled in these words. (*kn, gn, n*)
- Can your child think of any other words that contain the /n/ sound? (e.g. *nut, gnat, knife*)

Extending vocabulary
- Show your child the following pair of words. Explain that they are antonyms (opposites):
- dangerous / safe
- Ask them if they can think of an antonym for each of the following words:

  cool (*warm/hot*)   stops (*starts*)   find (*lose*)

  less (*more*)   stronger (*weaker*)   fastest (*slowest*)